# Queen Elizabeth II

## MODERN MONARCH

# Queen Elizabeth II
## MODERN MONARCH

**MATT DOEDEN**

LERNER PUBLICATIONS ◆ MINNEAPOLIS

Lerner Publications Company
An imprint of Lerner Publishing Group, Inc.
241 First Avenue North
Minneapolis, MN 55401 USA

For reading levels and more information, look up this title at www.lernerbooks.com.

Image credits: Mark Cuthbert/Getty Images, p. 2; Joe Giddens/PA Images/Getty Images, p. 6; Popperfoto/Getty Images, pp. 8, 18–20; Hulton Archive/Getty Images, p. 9; Central Press / Getty Images, p. 10; Lisa Sherida/Studio Lisa/Getty Images, pp. 11, 13; Ann Ronan Pictures/ Print Collector/Getty Images, p. 12; Evening Standard/Getty Images, p. 14; Hulton-Deutsch Collection/CORBIS/Getty Images, p. 15; Fox Photos/Hulton Archive/Getty Images, pp. 16, 30; Samir Hussein/WireImage/Getty Images, p. 17; Topical Press Agency/Hulton Archive/Getty Images, p. 21; Keystone/Getty Images, p. 22; Bettmann/Getty Images, pp. 23–24; J. A. Hampton/ Topical Press Agency/Getty Images, p. 25; Imagno/Getty Images, p. 27; The Print Collector/Getty Images, p. 28; Trinity Mirror/Mirrorpix/Alamy Stock Photo, p. 29; Tim Graham/Getty Images, pp. 31, 34; Graham Wiltshire/Getty Images, p. 32; Terry Fincher/Princess Diana Archive/Getty Images, p. 33; ALASTAIR GRANT/AFP/Getty Images, p. 36; Max Mumby/Indigo/Getty Images, p. 39. Cover: Paul Marriott/Alamy Stock Photo.

Main body text set in Rotis Serif Std 55 Regular.
Typeface provided by Adobe Systems.

Library of Congress Cataloging-in-Publication Data

Names: Doeden, Matt, author.
Title: Queen Elizabeth II : modern monarch / Matt Doeden.
Other titles: Queen Elizabeth the Second
Description: Minneapolis : Lerner Publications, 2020. | Series: Gateway biographies | Includes bibliographical references and index. | Audience: Ages 9–14 | Audience: Grades 4–6 | Summary: "Queen Elizabeth II is the longest-reigning British monarch. Discover more engaging details of her life and how she brought the royal family into the twenty-first century"– Provided by publisher.
Identifiers: LCCN 2019028056 (print) | LCCN 2019028057 (ebook) | ISBN 9781541577442 (library binding) | ISBN 9781541588905 (paperback) | ISBN 9781541583085 (ebook)
Subjects: LCSH: Elizabeth II, Queen of Great Britain, 1926– —Juvenile literature. | Queens—Great Britain—Biography—Juvenile literature.
Classification: LCC DA590 .D64 2020  (print) | LCC DA590  (ebook) | DDC 941.085092 [B]—dc23

LC record available at https://lccn.loc.gov/2019028056
LC ebook record available at https://lccn.loc.gov/2019028057

Manufactured in the United States of America
1-46767-47758-8/30/2019

# CONTENTS

Queen Elizabeth II visits Cambridge in 2019.

Millions of people lined the streets of London, England, on June 2, 1953. They gathered from Buckingham Palace to Westminster Abbey, eager to catch a glimpse of twenty-seven-year-old Queen Elizabeth II as she prepared for one of the biggest days of her life, her coronation. It celebrated her new reign as queen of the United Kingdom and the other Commonwealth countries.

Eight gray horses pulled the royal coach that carried Elizabeth and her family along the procession route. Elizabeth wore a white satin dress embroidered with the floral emblems of the Commonwealth countries. She wore the George IV State Diadem, an ornate crown adorned in gold, silver, diamonds, and pearls.

Once the coach reached Westminster Abbey, the ceremony began and lasted almost three hours. More than eight thousand guests, including heads of state from around the Commonwealth, watched as Elizabeth

Crowds watch Queen Elizabeth II's coach along the procession route.

prepared to take her oaths. Millions more listened on their radios or watched on television. It was the first coronation ceremony ever to be broadcast on live TV. Elizabeth was the center of attention as she vowed to serve all people of the British Empire.

"Throughout all my life and with all my heart I shall strive to be worthy of your trust," she promised.

The ceremony reached a high point as Geoffrey Fisher, the Archbishop of Canterbury, placed St Edward's Crown—the official coronation crown—on

Elizabeth's head. The crowd gathered in Westminster Abbey chanted, "God Save the Queen" as a 21-gun salute was fired from the Tower of London 3 miles (5 km) away.

After returning to Buckingham Palace, Elizabeth thrilled onlookers by appearing on the palace's balcony to wave to the people gathered outside. Fireworks filled the sky as the celebration continued through the day and into the night. Queen Elizabeth's reign had begun. It would be the longest reign in the history of the British monarchs.

Elizabeth wears St Edward's Crown after her coronation.

# Born a Princess

Princess Elizabeth Alexandra Mary Windsor was born April 21, 1926, in London, England. Elizabeth was born into England's royal family. Her grandfather was King George V, monarch of the British Empire. Historically, British monarchs had held a great deal of power over the nation, but by this time, the monarch's political power was limited. Elizabeth's parents were Prince Albert, Duke of York, and Lady Elizabeth Bowes-Lyon. Yet when she was born, there was little reason to believe Elizabeth would ever become queen. Her father, Albert, was the king's second son. Her uncle Edward was next in line to become king.

Elizabeth with her parents in 1926

Elizabeth (*left*) with her parents and sister, Margaret

As a child, Elizabeth went by the name Lilibet, which was how she first pronounced her name. She grew up living the privileged life of a royal, spending her time in places such as the Royal Lodge and Windsor Great Park. When Elizabeth was four, a second daughter, Margaret, was born.

Elizabeth was a mischievous and imaginative child. At one royal function, she was reported to have pelted guests with crackers. She was prone to rudely pointing out others' flaws, especially in their appearance. And after a disagreement with one of her tutors, Elizabeth picked up an inkpot and dumped it over her own head. Her cousin recalled that she liked to pretend that she was a pony. She would become so engrossed in her play that she wouldn't even respond when called. "I couldn't answer you as a pony," she reasoned.

Elizabeth grew up in love with horses. She was even given a Shetland pony named Peggy when she was four years old. As soon as she could read, she read books about horses. At night she would sit on her bed, pretending to drive a team of horses around the park. "I mostly go once or twice around the park before I go to sleep, you know," she said when asked what she was doing. "It exercises my horses."

**Elizabeth riding her horse**

Elizabeth with her corgis, Jane and Dookie

Elizabeth also grew to love dogs. Her father brought her on a hunting trip, where she played with his Welsh corgis. She got her first corgi, named Dookie, in 1933. It began a lifelong love for the breed.

But royal life also had its drawbacks. Elizabeth was often sheltered from the rest of the world. She didn't go to school. Instead, she and Margaret were taught at home. They learned about reading, writing, music, and current events. Elizabeth learned to speak French. She also spent time in the Girl Guides, a youth group similar to the Girl Scouts.

# Big Changes

Elizabeth's grandfather, King George V, was in poor health. He had suffered an injury during World War I (1914–1918) and also suffered from lung problems, probably due to a lifetime of heavy smoking. He died in 1936, when Elizabeth was ten. Her uncle, Edward VIII, took over as king.

Edward had been a popular king, but he caused an uproar when he fell in love with an American woman named Wallis Simpson. Simpson had been married twice already. When Edward proposed to Simpson later that year, it caused controversy. As king, Edward was the official head of the Church of England. The church strongly disapproved of the king marrying a divorced woman.

Edward knew that he could not marry Simpson while he was king. So he gave up his throne, an act called abdication.

**King Edward VIII with Wallis Simpson**

**Princess Elizabeth (*second from left*) with family on her father, King George VI's, coronation**

His shocking decision had a huge impact on Elizabeth. When Edward gave up the throne, Prince Albert became king. Monarchs traditionally took on new names when they ascended to the throne. Albert chose to follow in his father's footsteps, becoming King George VI. As the king's oldest child, Elizabeth was suddenly next in line to become queen. Princess Elizabeth's future changed dramatically. She was preparing to become one of the most influential people in the world.

It was a time of change for the royal family. It was also a time of change in Europe. On the European continent, fears were growing about the rise of the Nazi Party in Germany. The Nazis, led by Chancellor Adolf Hitler, spread hate about many groups of people, most notably those of Jewish ancestry. When Germany invaded Poland in 1939, World War II (1939–1945) began. Britain, France, and other nations took up arms against Germany. Thirteen-year-old Elizabeth watched as Europe fell into war.

Many people fled London. Germany had a powerful air force, and it wasn't long until German bomber planes were soaring over the British Isles. The king feared for the safety of his girls. As king, he had to stay at Buckingham Palace. But he knew that the palace was a target for

Elizabeth's parents, King George VI and Queen Elizabeth, survey bomb damage to Buckingham Palace in 1940.

**Princesses Elizabeth and Margaret lived at Windsor Castle during part of World War II.**

German bombers. So he sent them to Windsor Castle, near London. The castle was a fortress, and the king hoped the girls would be safe there. Elizabeth and Margaret spent more than five years separated from their parents as the war raged on. The castle's windows were blacked out so that no one could see inside. The castle was surrounded by barbed wire and protected with weapons designed to shoot down German aircraft. It was a gloomy way for Elizabeth to spend her teenage years.

Meanwhile, Elizabeth continued her education. She was

**Elizabeth (*right*) prepares to give her first speech.**

preparing to become queen one day. She knew that she would have to be a leader. In 1940, at the age of fourteen, she gave her first public speech, by radio.

"Thousands of you in this country have had to leave your homes and be separated from your fathers and mothers," she said. "My sister Margaret Rose and I feel so much for you as we know from experience what it means to be away from those we love most of all. . . . We know, every one of us, that in the end all will be well; for God will care for us and give us victory and peace. And when peace comes, remember it will be for us, the children of today, to make the world of tomorrow a better and happier place."

# MILITARY SERVICE

When Elizabeth turned eighteen, she enlisted in the Women's Auxiliary Territorial Service (ATS), even though her father advised her against it. She served as a mechanic and was the only head of state to serve in World War II. She learned how to change truck wheels, rebuild engines, and drive vehicles such as ambulances. She enjoyed the chance to work with her hands and proudly showed off grease stains on her hands and dirt under her nails as proof that she was working hard.

Princess Elizabeth shows her mother, Queen Elizabeth, her mechanical work.

People line the streets of London to celebrate the end of World War II.

## Marriage and Family

As Elizabeth came into adulthood, she took on more and more responsibilities. In 1943, the British Parliament passed a law allowing her to act as a Counsellor of State at the age of eighteen instead of twenty-one. Counsellors of State are members of the royal family who can conduct official business and speak on behalf of the monarch.

When the war in Europe ended in 1945 with the defeat of Germany, the people of Britain took to the streets for a massive celebration. Elizabeth and Margaret had long been sheltered from the wider world. But they wanted to be a part of the celebration. So they went into the crowd. No one recognized the princesses, which allowed them to move through the crowd freely and experience the joy without being the center of attention. "We cheered the

King and Queen on the balcony and then walked miles through the streets," Elizabeth later recalled. "I remember lines of unknown people linking arms and walking . . . all of us just swept along on a tide of happiness and relief."

The war was over, and life slowly returned to normal. Elizabeth had been a child when the fighting started. But by the time it was over, she was a young woman. As a teenager, Elizabeth had met Prince Philip, a member of both the Danish and Greek royal families. The two had hit it off. They exchanged letters. After the war, the two began a courtship. They announced their engagement in 1947.

**Princess Elizabeth and Prince Philip after announcing their engagement**

**Elizabeth and Philip on their wedding day**

The announcement was not popular with many in Great Britain. Philip was not born in Britain. His sisters had married German men with ties to the Nazi Party. Some felt that Philip was not a proper match for the future queen. According to one newspaper poll at the time, 40 percent of British people opposed the wedding. But Elizabeth made her own decision.

The couple was married on November 20, 1947, in Westminster Abbey. It was an extravagant ceremony at a time when Britain's economy was still recovering from the war. Elizabeth wore an ivory wedding gown made of silk, sewn with thousands of small pearls. They invited two thousand people to the wedding. Among the guests were some of the world's wealthiest and most powerful people, including six kings and seven queens.

After the celebration, the couple went to Hampshire for a honeymoon. While in Hampshire, Elizabeth dressed in army boots and a leather jacket so she could look for wild deer with her new husband. She wrote to her sister that she felt "like a female Russian commando leader followed by her ever-faithful cut-throats."

Less than a year later, on November 14, 1948, the couple welcomed their first child, Prince Charles. When Prince Philip first saw Charles he said he looked like "a plum pudding." Not long after, they moved from Buckingham Palace to Clarence House. Repairs were needed on Buckingham Palace for the damage from World War II. At Clarence House, Elizabeth and Philip had a second child. Princess Anne was born on August 15, 1950. The family of four was excited for their next chapter.

Elizabeth and her family enjoying a picnic

# My Own Name, of Course

By 1951 Elizabeth's father was in poor health. King George VI struggled with several serious diseases, including lung cancer. As the king's health grew worse, Elizabeth took on more and more of his duties. That year she and Philip toured Canada. They met with heads of state but also took in the sights, which Elizabeth happily filmed with her video camera. From there, they traveled to the United States, where they visited US president Harry S. Truman in Washington, DC. Truman was impressed by young Elizabeth, saying everyone that met her fell in love with her.

In February 1952, Elizabeth stepped in for her father on an official state visit to New Zealand and Australia. The king went to the airport to see Elizabeth and Philip

Elizabeth visiting President Harry S. Truman

King George VI and Queen Elizabeth leave the plane after saying goodbye to Princess Elizabeth.

off on their journey, which would begin in Kenya. King George VI and Queen Elizabeth gave their daughter a private farewell on the plane. Then the king waved to Elizabeth and Philip from the tarmac as the plane took off.

It would be the last time Elizabeth would ever see her father. A week later, she was in Kenya, excitedly filming the nation's diverse wildlife with her video camera, when Philip brought her the news. Her father had died. It was Elizabeth's turn to ascend to the throne. Many kings and queens take new names once they ascend. But when Elizabeth was asked what she would call herself, she had a simple answer. "My own name, of course. What else?" That made her Queen Elizabeth II. The first Queen Elizabeth ruled from 1558 to 1603.

Elizabeth and Philip quickly flew back to London for the king's funeral. Elizabeth had been preparing for this moment most of her life. She was ready to step up and take on the responsibilities as queen. "It was all very sudden," Elizabeth later recalled. "Kind of taking it on, making the best job you can. It's a question of maturing into something one's got used to doing, and accepting the fact that you are here, and it's your fate."

Elizabeth immediately got to work, meeting with world leaders. She had always worked to overcome her shyness. But in her new role, Elizabeth surprised herself with her comfort and confidence. "Extraordinary thing," she said, "I no longer feel anxious or worried. I don't know what it is, but I have lost all my timidity."

A little more than a year later, in June 1953, Elizabeth was officially crowned in her coronation ceremony. Millions across the Commonwealth and around the world watched the ceremony on TV. Elizabeth's reign began just as communication and media were becoming increasingly global. The royal family, with her at the center of it, was a source of fascination and curiosity. The public eye was continually on her, a difficult position for someone naturally shy and reserved.

## Changing Times

The early part of Elizabeth's reign was a time of change, both personally and globally. The British Empire, in which Great Britain ruled foreign states, was dissolving. It was

# QUEEN ELIZABETH I

Queen Elizabeth I ruled England from 1558 until her death in 1603. Elizabeth did not have an easy path to the throne. She was born to King Henry VIII and Anne Boleyn. The king wanted a son, and he had Elizabeth's mother executed when Elizabeth was just three years old. As a young woman, Elizabeth spent a year in prison on suspicion of helping rebels that supported the Protestant religion. Her role in the rebellion was unclear, but Elizabeth was in favor of reducing the power of the Roman Catholic Church, which made her a threat to many Catholics in power.

After the deaths of her brother Edward in 1553 and sister Mary in 1558, Elizabeth ascended to the throne. She was largely a beloved ruler, especially among her Protestant subjects. She helped build England into a world power. She reestablished the Church of England, which remains a big part of the nation's modern identity.

being replaced with the Commonwealth of Nations, a more cooperative organization of former British territories. In 1953–1954, Elizabeth embarked on a seven-month tour, visiting thirteen countries. They included New Zealand and Australia—the nations she had planned to visit a year earlier before her father's death.

As queen, Elizabeth's role was largely diplomatic. She did not make laws. Instead, she worked to ensure cooperation throughout the Commonwealth. Her calm but tough manner was well suited to the task. Elizabeth spent much of her time either traveling or hosting heads of state.

For more than half a decade, Elizabeth remained devoted mainly to her role as queen. She carved out time

The countries in red were part of the British Empire in 1902. The Commonwealth consists of 53 countries, including Canada, Australia, and India.

Elizabeth crowned Charles Prince of Wales and Earl of Chester in 1969.

in the day to spend with her children, including helping with their baths and bedtimes, but she was often busy on official business. Her family returned to center stage, however, with the birth of two sons, Andrew in 1959 and Edward in 1963.

As Elizabeth's heir, Prince Charles was often the center of attention for the media. In 1969 Elizabeth crowned her oldest son as Prince of Wales and Earl of Chester, giving him a seat in Britain's House of Lords. Elizabeth supported Charles as he attended the University of Cambridge and served in both the Royal Air Force and the Royal Navy.

By the late 1960s, media coverage was changing the way people thought about the royal family. Elizabeth and her family often seemed distant and separate from the rest of the population. In 1969 Elizabeth agreed to allow a camera crew into Buckingham Palace to film the family's daily life.

The documentary *Royal Family*, filmed in 1969, showed Elizabeth and her family's home life.

The documentary, *Royal Family*, was a massive success. An estimated forty million people watched it in Great Britain alone. Elizabeth appeared comfortable and witty, helping to improve her image with her subjects. It was a risky move, but it came with largely positive results for the royal family.

## The Next Generation

As Elizabeth's children grew into adulthood, her role gradually changed. She took on more of the role of an adviser. Elizabeth and Anne talked passionately about horses. She helped the youngest boys with their schoolwork. Andrew dreamed of studying abroad, while Edward played several school sports.

However, it was not always easy to be in the public eye. More and more, Charles and his siblings became the center of media attention. Elizabeth did not always agree with her children and sometimes did not hide her disapproval.

The royal family experienced a frightening crisis in 1974. Princess Anne and her husband, Mark Phillips, were heading home to Buckingham Palace from a charity event. Suddenly, a car forced them to pull over. A man rushed out from the car, armed with guns. He was attempting to kidnap the princess.

The attacker fired several shots, hitting Anne's personal police officer, James Beaton. He also shot her driver, a police officer, and a motorist. He ordered Anne to get out of the car. "Bloody likely!" she responded, refusing to get out.

Help soon arrived, and the attacker was arrested. Everyone who had been shot in the attack recovered. A near disaster was averted, but it was a major scare for Elizabeth and her family. Later that year, Elizabeth awarded Beaton the George Cross, Britain's highest

Princess Anne is known for her cool temper even in a crisis.

civilian medal. "The medal is from the Queen of England, the thank you is from Anne's mother," she told him.

Life went on for the royal family as the children went on to start families of their own. Anne had married Phillips in 1973. In 1977, the couple welcomed their first child and Elizabeth's first grandchild, Peter Phillips.

That year Britain marked the twenty-fifth anniversary of Elizabeth's coronation. The celebration was called the Silver Jubilee, and Elizabeth traveled all around the Commonwealth. The party came at a time when the nation's economy was struggling. Elizabeth was concerned that people would not be in favor of an expensive party. But the celebration, capped off by Jubilee Days in June, was a hit.

Queen Elizabeth II visits an admiring crowd during her Silver Jubilee celebration.

Prince Charles and Princess Diana on their wedding day in 1981

## A Princess and an Heir

In 1981 Prince Charles announced his engagement to Lady Diana Spencer. Charles was thirty-two years old, and pressure had been mounting for him to settle down and begin a family. Spencer had ties to the royal family. She was intelligent, charitable, and seemed like the perfect fit. Elizabeth approved of the match.

The wedding was held at St Paul's Cathedral on July 29, 1981. It was a grand ceremony watched by an estimated 750 million people on television. Diana moved into Kensington Palace. But she found life there troubling. She felt cut off and distressed. The marriage was not going well. Elizabeth often spoke with Diana, doing her best to comfort her daughter-in-law.

It didn't take long for Charles and Diana to produce an heir. Their first child, Prince William, was born on June 21, 1982. As the world celebrated the birth of a future king, Elizabeth was hopeful that the baby would help close the gap that had opened between Charles and Diana. A second prince, Harry, followed in 1984. The little boys were media sensations. But the cold relationship between Diana and Charles continued. As time passed, Elizabeth became less and less sympathetic toward Diana.

The relationship between the women reached a breaking point in 1992. Author Andrew Morton published a biography of Diana that painted the royal family in a harsh light. Elizabeth blamed Diana for letting her friends work with the author.

Charles and Diana at home with their son, William

It seemed clear to many that the marriage was doomed. Charles was in love with another woman, Camilla Parker Bowles. Diana wanted her freedom. Elizabeth did all she could to keep it together, ordering a six-month cooling-off period. But it didn't help. A fairy-tale wedding had not produced a fairy-tale marriage.

When the situation didn't get better, she sent letters to Charles and Diana, asking them to divorce. They agreed. Their divorce was finalized in 1996. Diana was beloved in Great Britain and around the world. She was praised for her charitable work and likable personality. The split with Charles reflected poorly on the royal family, and on Elizabeth.

Life went on, however. Diana was free to live her own life, but she remained the mother of William and Harry and was very much in the public spotlight.

A year later, Diana was killed in a car accident. The nation, and the world, mourned her loss. Elizabeth addressed the nation. "[Diana] was an exceptional and gifted human being," she said. "In good times and in bad, she never lost her capacity to smile and laugh, nor to inspire others with her warmth and kindness. I admired and respected her—for her energy and commitment to others, and especially for her devotion to her two boys."

Despite her words, many criticized the queen for seeming cold when addressing Diana's death. Some in the press vilified Charles, Elizabeth, and the royal family. It was one of the darkest times in Elizabeth's long reign.

Charles and Camilla on their wedding day in 2005

Charles married Camilla in 2005. It was a small ceremony with no fanfare. Neither Elizabeth nor Philip attended the wedding. They went to the reception, but friction between Charles and Elizabeth over his relationship with Camilla was no secret. Prince William stood with his father, acting as a witness to the union.

## The Longest Reign

Elizabeth remained on the throne as William and Harry grew into adulthood. Her health remained strong into her seventies and eighties, and she continued her lifelong passion for traveling the world.

In 2012, Elizabeth's Diamond Jubilee marked her sixtieth year on the throne. Elizabeth wrote a message to her subjects, reaffirming her pledge to serve.

"In this special year," she wrote, "as I dedicate myself anew to your service, I hope we will all be reminded of the power of togetherness and the convening strength of family, friendship and good neighbourliness, examples of which I have been fortunate to see throughout my reign and which my family and I look forward to seeing in many forms as we travel throughout the United Kingdom and the wider Commonwealth.

"I hope also that this Jubilee year will be a time to give thanks for the great advances that have been made since 1952 and to look forward to the future with clear head and warm heart as we join together in our celebrations."

Elizabeth has long been known for her serious and witty demeanor. But when the 2012 Summer Olympic Games came to London, she had a little fun. She played herself in a skit with James Bond actor Daniel Craig in which she boards a helicopter which takes her to the opening ceremony. The short film was played at the ceremony, showing the queen (played by a stunt double) jumping out of the helicopter and parachuting down before making a big entrance to officially open the games. In 2013, the British Academy of Film and Television Arts (BAFTA) gave the queen an honorary award, calling her the most memorable Bond girl yet.

Meanwhile, Elizabeth looked on as her grandchildren married and began new generations of the royal family. In 2011, Prince William married Kate Middleton. Middleton, who became the Duchess of Cambridge, was massively popular and helped spark a renewed interest in the royal family. Elizabeth welcomed Kate to the family with open arms, and the two enjoy a warm relationship, often appearing together at public events.

William and Kate thrilled Elizabeth with a great-grandson in 2013. Prince George became third in line to the throne, behind Charles and William. Months after Elizabeth became the longest reigning British monarch, she had another reason to celebrate. William and Kate had a daughter, Princess Charlotte, in 2015, and another son, Prince Louis, in 2018.

The family kept growing. In 2018, Prince Harry married American actress Meghan Markle. A year later, their son, Archie Mountbatten-Windsor, was born. Archie was Elizabeth's eighth great-grandchild and is seventh in line to the throne.

## The Future

In April 2019, Elizabeth celebrated her ninety-third birthday. Although her health was good, age had begun to slow her down. Some have wondered whether Elizabeth will abdicate her throne, clearing the way for Prince

William, Kate, and their three children celebrate Elizabeth's ninety-third birthday.

Charles to become king. But many experts on the royal family believe that it's unlikely Elizabeth will do so. Her uncle Edward remains the only British monarch that chose to abdicate the throne.

Instead, Elizabeth has been gradually handing over more and more royal duties to Charles. She is already making fewer public appearances than in years past. In 2018, she said that she would step down as head of the Commonwealth, letting Charles take over those duties.

# LINE OF SUCCESSION

The order in which members of the royal family are in line to become monarch is called the line of succession. The rules that govern this line have been in place for more than 300 years. The heir apparent, or first in line, is the eldest child of the reigning monarch. From there, it moves down the line to the heir's children, followed by children of the heir's siblings. Here's a look at the line of succession as it stood in 2019.

Queen Elizabeth
1) Charles, Prince of Wales
2) Prince William, Duke of Cambridge
3) Prince George of Cambridge
4) Princess Charlotte of Cambridge
5) Prince Louis of Cambridge
6) Prince Harry, Duke of Sussex
7) Archie Mountbatten-Windsor
8) Prince Andrew, Duke of York
9) Princess Beatrice of York
10) Princess Eugenie of York
11) Prince Edward, Earl of Wessex
12) James, Viscount Severn
13) Lady Louise Windsor
14) Anne, the Princess Royal
15) Peter Phillips
16) Savannah Phillips
17) Isla Phillips
18) Zara Tindall
19) Mia Tindall
20) Lena Tindall

Elizabeth meets Harry and Meghan's son, Archie.

When Elizabeth was born, she was not destined for the throne. Yet she has reigned for almost seven decades—the longest in the history of the monarchy. She has helped to guide Great Britain through times of tremendous change and uncertainty. She has stood as a symbol of Great Britain's past while helping to lead the royal family into a new era. Her legacy will live on through her children, grandchildren, and great-grandchildren.

# IMPORTANT DATES

1926    Elizabeth is born on April 21 in London, England.

1936    Elizabeth's father becomes king when his brother abdicates the throne. Elizabeth becomes heir to the throne.

1939    World War II begins. Elizabeth and her sister live at Windsor Castle, separated from their parents.

1940    Elizabeth gives her first public speech, by radio.

1945    World War II ends. Elizabeth and her sister take to the streets, unrecognized, to join the celebration.

1947    Elizabeth marries Prince Philip.

1948    Elizabeth gives birth to her first child, Prince Charles.

1952    King George VI dies. Elizabeth becomes queen.

1953    Elizabeth is formally crowned in a coronation ceremony at Westminster Abbey.

1969    Elizabeth allows a documentary, titled *Royal Family*, to be filmed at Buckingham Palace.

**1974** A plot to kidnap Elizabeth's daughter Anne fails.

**1977** Great Britain celebrates Elizabeth's Silver Jubilee.

**1982** Prince Charles marries Lady Diana Spencer.

**1983** Prince William is born.

**1996** Charles and Diana divorce.

**1997** Diana is killed in a car accident.

**2007** Elizabeth becomes the longest-reigning royal in Britain's history.

**2019** Elizabeth celebrates her ninety-third birthday. She continues to hand over more and more of her royal duties to Charles.

# SOURCE NOTES

8   "1953: Queen Elizabeth takes Coronation Oath," BBC, June 2, 1953, http://news.bbc.co.uk/onthisday/hi/dates/stories/june/2/newsid_2654000/2654501.stm.

12  Sally Bedell Smith, *Elizabeth the Queen: Inside the Life of a Modern Monarch* (New York: Random House, 2012), p. 4.

12  Carolly Erickson, *Lilibet: An Intimate Portrait of Elizabeth II* (New York: St. Martin's Griffin, 2004), p. 24.

18  "First Speech of Princess Elizabeth, the Future Queen," Forces War Records, October 13, 2016, https://www.forces-war-records.co.uk/blog/2016/10/13/first-speech-of-princess-elizabeth-the-future-queen.

20–21  Richard Palmer, "The Queen will Celebrate the 70th Anniversary of VE Day at Westminster Abbey," *Express*, April 3, 2015, https://www.express.co.uk/news/royal/568133/Queen-70th-anniversary-VE-Day-Westminster-Abbey.

23  Smith, *Elizabeth the Queen*, p. 43.

23  Brian McGleenon, "The Reason Why Prince Charles Was 'Frightened' of Prince Philip Who 'Only Tolerated Him,'" *Express*, June 13, 2019.

25  Smith, *Elizabeth the Queen*, p. 65.

26  Smith, *Elizabeth the Queen*, p. 65.

26  Smith, *Elizabeth the Queen*, p. 67.

31  Carrie Hagen, "The Bloody Attempt to Kidnap a British Princess." Smithsonian. 20 March 2014. https://www.smithsonianmag.com/history/bloody-attempt-kidnap-british-princess-180950202/.

32  Hagen, "Bloody Attempt."

35 Kayla Keegan. "A Closer Look at Queen Elizabeth II and Princess Diana's Complicated Relationship." Good Housekeeping. Jun 24, 2019. https://www.goodhousekeeping.com/life/a23363409/queen -elizabeth-princess-diana-relationship/.

37 "The Queen's Diamond Jubilee Message." February 6, 2012. https://www.royal.uk/queens-diamond-jubilee-message.

# SELECTED BIBLIOGRAPHY

Bilyeau, Nancy and Chanel Vargas. "The Story of Queen Elizabeth's Wedding Day," *Town & Country*, May 18, 2018. https://www .townandcountrymag.com/leisure/arts-and-culture/news/a8451/queen -elizabeth-prince-philip-wedding/.

Erickson, Carolly. *Lilibet: An Intimate Portrait of Elizabeth II*, New York: St. Martin's Griffin, 2004.

The Home of the Royal Family https://www.royal.uk/.

Keegan, Kayla. "Inside Queen Elizabeth II and Princess Diana's Very Complicated Relationship," Good Housekeeping, September 22, 2018. https://www.goodhousekeeping.com/life/a23363409/queen-elizabeth -princess-diana-relationship/.

Ryan, Catherine. *The Queen: The Life and Times of Elizabeth II*. New York: Chartwell Books, 2017.

Seward, Ingrid. "The Truth About Queen Elizabeth II and Princess Diana's Relationship," Reader's Digest, August 2001. https://www. rd.com/culture/queen-elizabeth-princess-diana-truth-relationship/.

Smith, Sally Bedell. *Elizabeth the Queen: The Life of a Modern Monarch*. New York: Random House, 2013.

# FURTHER READING

## BOOKS

Ribke, Simone T. *William and Kate: The Prince and Princess*. New York: Children's Press, 2016.
　Follow the lives, romance, and marriage of England's most famous couple.

Sherman, Jill. *Prince Harry & Meghan: Royals for a New Era*. Minneapolis: Lerner Publications, 2019.
　People worldwide are fascinated with this power couple. Find out more about who they are, how they met, and how they fit into the royal family.

Zeiger, Jennifer. *Queen Elizabeth II*. New York: Children's Press, 2016.
　This easy-reading biography tracks the life and reign of Queen Elizabeth II.

## WEBSITES

The Home of the Royal Family
　https://www.royal.uk/
　The official site of the royal family offers profiles, news, and photos of Queen Elizabeth and her family.

How Royalty Works
　https://history.howstuffworks.com/historical-figures/royalty.htm
　What is royalty? How does it work around the globe and throughout history? Learn more about kings, queens, princes, and princesses.

*National Geographic Kids*: 15 Fun Facts about the Queen
　https://www.natgeokids.com/uk/discover/history/monarchy/facts -about-the-queen-elizabeth-ii/
　Learn more about Queen Elizabeth II with this fun, easy-to-read list.

# INDEX